First Stories

Judy Lunsford

Copyright Information

Rumtuskin of the Emberdiggers
Copyright © 2020 by Judy Lunsford
Cover and layout copyright © by Judy Lunsford
Cover art copyright © john1279/depositphotos.com
and ©lenmdp/depositphotos.com

Reality Fails
Copyright © 2021 by Judy Lunsford
Cover and layout copyright © by Judy Lunsford
Cover art copyright © majcot/depositphotos.com

Shandoah
Copyright © 2020 by Judy Lunsford
Cover and layout copyright © by Judy Lunsford &
Don Williamson
Cover art copyright © wenani/depositphotos.com

Moon Songs
Copyright © 2018 by Judy Lunsford
Cover and layout copyright © by Judy Lunsford
Cover art copyright © LAN02/shutterstock.com

Aeris Awakens
Copyright © Judy Lunsford 2020
Cover photo copyright © prometeus/depositphotos

This book is licensed for your personal enjoyment only. All rights reserved. This is a work of fiction. All characters and events portrayed in this book are fictional, and any resemblance to real people or incidents is purely coincidental. This book, or parts thereof, may not be reproduced in any form without permission.

Table of Contents

Introduction

This collection is filled with the first short stories that go along with stories from other series. It is a great introduction to some of my series if you are a first-time reader.

Included in this collection are the Crystal Tower series (*Rumtuskin of the Emberdiggers*); the Fahlstrom adventures (*Reality Fails*); the Fire Lily trilogy (*Shandoah*); the Moon Songs series (*Moon Songs*); and the Wild Hunt trilogy (*Aeris Awakens*).

Each story will be preceded by a brief introduction and a little bit about the series it comes from.

At the time of this publication, some of these series were finished, some weren't. I am working hard to finish all of the series that I have slated to publish over the next few years.

I hope you find something you like.
Happy reading!

Judy Lunsford
March 2021

Rumtuskin of the Emberdiggers

A Crystal Tower short story

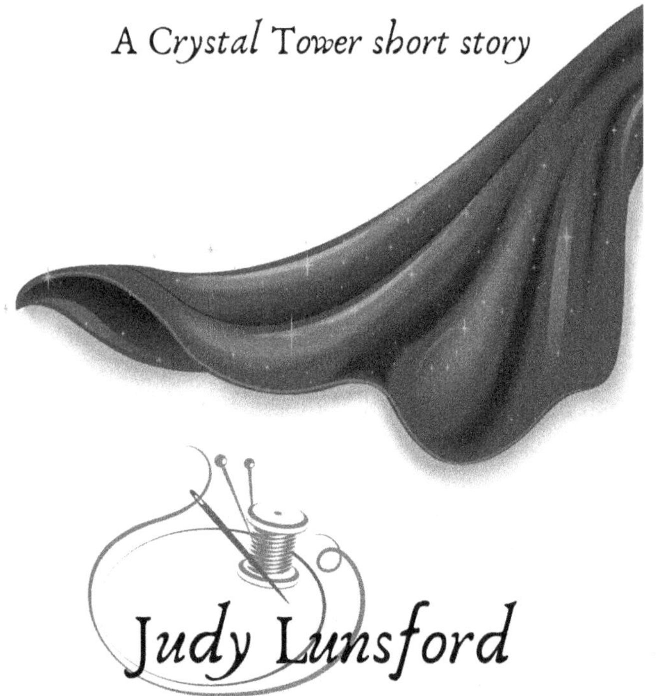

Judy Lunsford

Rumtuskin of the Emberdiggers

Chronologically, this is the first short story written so far (as of March 2021) for the Crystal Tower series. Short stories are currently available, novels are yet to be released at the publishing of this collection. The series covers the epic fantasy of the royal family of Shal Tahl and the dragons that are bonded to the family. This is an introduction to some of the main characters from the middle of the epic saga.

The purple velvet tree was highly sought after by magicians and sorcerers everywhere. This made life complicated for them. Burble was no exception.

His beautifully hued leaves were the softest foliage available. Softer than any fabric made by human hands. They had a faint scent of the forest to them, one which could never be overpowered by any other odor.

His leaves were also very susceptible to magic. Burble's delicate leaves were perfect for spells, potions, and charms. But the best magic was tailor magic.

Clothing made from the leaves of the purple velvet tree were seamless and durable and the most comfortable cloth. They did not rip or tear easily and were almost strong enough to be a light layer of armor.

Burble had many brushes with velvet hunters. He was defenseless, for the most part. He moved rather slowly, usually tripping himself on his own roots, which were shallow enough that he could move across the ground with fair, if slow, ease.

The main defense of the purple velvet trees were their symbiotes. A long vine of ivy wrapped itself around the trunk of every velvet tree. But it wasn't any common ivy. It was a crawling attack ivy.

Burble's symbiote was named Crawl. But the symbiote did more than crawl. He was faster than lightning, and he had no qualms about strangling any hunter that came too close to Burble. The ivy was also stronger than iron chains, almost impossible to break without a tremendous amount of strength.

The symbiote ivy lived off the sap produced by the purple velvet tree. It was their only source of food. And the sap was toxic to the purple velvet tree. Without a crawling ivy, the purple velvet trees would die. Without a tree, the ivy would die. So, Crawl had good reason to protect Burble with his life.

Crawl had been with Burble for as long as he could remember. Crawling ivy finds young velvet trees almost instinctively. And they are joined for life. They both have exceptionally long lifespans, so they have centuries together.

Burble was unique, even among the other purple velvet trees. He had allergies. And the thing he was most allergic to was himself. Or he thought he was. Burble was also a hypochondriac.

Burble would sneeze if his leaves came too close to his trunk. Usually with drooping leaves like a weeping willow, velvet trees had long flowing wispy branches that fell around them gracefully like a veil. But Burble kept his branches held away from himself, lest the velvet brush against his bark in a place where Crawl did not serve as protection.

Burble was a rather young tree. He was looking forward to his eighty-fifth spring. He and Crawl always celebrated by going to a special lake in the middle of the forest, where they were joined for the first time. It was a breeding ground for the purple velvet trees in the fall, but in mid-spring, it was usually frequented by the younger trees who still bothered to celebrate their birthday.

It was eerily quiet when they got there. Burble slowed his approach to the lake. The air was filled with the scent of the grass of the meadow, but not of any other velvet trees.

There were usually at least a few other velvet trees scattered around. It was a beautiful waterhole, surrounded by a small meadow where the velvet trees had an easy time moving around. The sounds of spring were normal, with birds singing, and small rabbits hopping here and there. Rabbits were particularly fond of velvet trees, and the meadow was usually full of them, with the baby rabbits hopping through the meadow to greet the velvet trees as they arrived.

But there were no birds singing, and the meadow was empty of rabbits. Not even one was to be seen.

"Where is everyone?" Burble asked.

"Get back into the woods," Crawl ordered. "Something is very wrong."

Burble started to move back towards the cover of the woods, but before he could get very far, it was already too late. An owlephant came lumbering through the meadow from a not far away.

Although rare in this part of the forest, owlephants did wander to the lake occasionally. The beast had the body and trunk of an elephant, but the head and wings of an owl. The talons on their bulbous feet were sharp enough to strip leaves and bark in a single swipe. An adult owlephant could knock over a velvet tree and pin them to the ground, rendering the tree helpless while made into a meal.

Burble stared in horror at the beast. Owlephants loved the leaves of the velvet trees. It was their favorite tasty snack. It caught sight of Burble and started to charge.

"Move," Crawl demanded. "I can't take it on myself. It's too big."

Burble started to move, but he wasn't fast enough. The huge beast caught up to them in seconds and Burble was nowhere near close enough to the trees to be able to escape from the owlephant.

It reached its trunk out to grab Burble by some branches as Crawl shot out and wrapped himself around the neck of the beast.

The owlephant reared back in shock and let out an ear-piercing roar. Crawl tried to tighten around the thick leathery skin where it met the feathers leading up to the creature's head. It was the only sweet spot that Crawl had to defeat the creature on his own.

Burble shrieked in horror and tried to pull away from the beast.

"Don't pull," Crawl demanded. "You're stretching me too much."

The elephant tried to lean away from Crawl, hoping to break his vine. Crawl held on around the beast's neck but didn't have the traction he needed to hold him. The owlephant reared back and Crawl lost his grip, giving the beast a chance to catch its breath.

But while the creature was still reared up, a dwarf came from out of nowhere. He hefted his spear and rammed it through the side of the soft flesh under the owlephant's armpit, where the feathers of the wing met the leathery skin and drove it sideways into the beast's heart.

The owlephant made the worst noise Burble had ever heard, shaking leaves from the trees above them, and then fell backwards with an earth quaking thud. It moved its legs a little, as reflexes tried to simulate escape, and then the beast lay quiet, the life gone from it forever.

The dwarf knelt by the beast's side. He removed his red hat and placed it over his heart as he bid the beast farewell. Dwarves took death very seriously and tried to never let their victims die alone. The only exception was in times of war, where there was no time for the dead.

Crawl tried to disentangle himself from around the beast's neck, but he was pinned to the ground on the underside.

When the dwarf was finished, he noticed Crawl trying to quietly escape while Burble tried to tilt the beast off his symbiote. The dwarf went and found a large stick and wedged it under the beast and used it as leverage to help the ivy free himself.

"Thank you for your assistance," Crawl said, once disentangled and once again wrapped safely around Burble's trunk.

"My pleasure," the dwarf said.

"We would offer you a reward for your bravery, but alas, we have nothing," Burble said politely.

"On the contrary," the dwarf said. "You have much that I need."

"You're a hunter?" Crawl bristled and was ready to attack again. "But dwarves have little interest in velvet trees."

"I am not a hunter," the dwarf said. "I am Rumtuskin of the Emberdiggers. I am a humble tailor."

The dwarf took off his hat and bowed deeply to Burble and Crawl. He straightened and smiled as he put his hat back into place.

"My name is Burble, and my ivy is Crawl," Burble said. "We are very grateful for your assistance. But we can't allow you to strip my leaves."

"I have no desire to strip your leaves," Rumtuskin said. "As I said, I am not a hunter."

"Then what do you want,' Crawl growled.

"I've been watching the two of you for some time," Rumtuskin said. "I have noticed that Burble tends to sneeze off his own leaves on a fairly regular basis."

"You've been following us?" Burble was amazed.

"How have I not sensed your presence?" Crawl demanded.

"I have stayed at a safe distance," Rumtuskin said. "I follow you far behind, and I collect the stray leaves from the ground."

Rumtuskin reached into a red leather pouch at his belt. He pulled out a piece of cloth, velvety and purple, obviously made from the leaves of velvet trees. It was seamless and beautiful.

"Oh, pretty," Burble cooed. "Is that made from me?"

"Yes," Rumtuskin smiled proudly. "If you would still like to offer a reward for my assistance, all I ask is that you allow me to travel with you. I will only pick up what falls naturally. But I will no longer have to chase the leaves in the breeze."

"Sure," Burble said cheerfully.

"No," Crawl said at the same time.

"Why not?" Burble asked.

"I don't trust him," Crawl said.

"But he saved us from the owlephant," Burble said. "And he was following us anyway."

"That's the part I don't like," Crawl said. "How do we know he isn't out to assassinate the King?"

"The King?" Rumtuskin asked. "Which King?"

"King DaeMark, of the Crystal Tower," Burble said.

"Don't tell him which King," Crawl tried to stop Burble but was too late.

"I can assure you that I am not an assassin," Rumtuskin said. "And if you are on your way to pay respects to the King, I will gladly wait behind at an encampment while you are there."

"You can come with us to meet the King," Burble said.

"No, he will wait for us," Crawl corrected. "The dwarves and the humans don't get along."

"King DaeMark gets along with everyone," Burble said.

"So that means I can come along with you?" Rumtuskin asked.

"For now," Crawl said. "But one wrong move and I will strangle you while you sleep."

"Agreed," Rumtuskin said happily.

Burble relaxed for the first time since he saw the owlephant and his branches accidentally brushed against his bark. He let out a loud sneeze and leaves rained down around them.

"Excuse me," Rumtuskin said. "That's my cue."

The dwarf scurried around and picked up every leaf and tucked them gently into his leather pouch.

"If you'd like, I can show you how I magic them together when we stop for the night," Rumtuskin said.

"Oh, I would like that very much," Burble squealed. "Very much indeed."

***

When the three reached a suitable campsite for the night, they stopped and started to make camp.

Burble and Crawl were used to just finding a place where Burble had enough space to rest for the night. But having a dwarf travelling with them made stopping for the night a little more complicated.

After passing three sites that Crawl thought were perfectly suitable, they finally found a place with a small clearing near a stream. Burble was happy to have water nearby and soaked his roots thoroughly.

They were surrounded securely by a nice assortment of trees and bushes, and the soft ground was covered with a nutritious moss for Burble.

Rumtuskin stopped and looked around the area and drew in a deep breath.

"Ah," he said. "I love the smell of the river moss. It reminds me of when I left the mountains with my mother to go gathering."

"You went gathering with your mother?" Crawl said. "I thought the dwarves lived within the mountains."

"We do," Rumtuskin said. "But my mother was half gnome. So, she liked to venture out of the mountain and into the woods. It made her feel more at home. The smells of the trees and flowers, the sounds of the birds. The feel of wet earth under her feet. The smell of rain. She needed all of that once in a while. Eventually, I did too."

"What did she gather?" Burble asked.

"Herbs, roots, and plants mostly," Rumtuskin said. "She was a healer, so she needed to replenish her supplies."

Crawl kept his eyes on Rumtuskin as he went about making camp.

Rumtuskin found a nice flat piece of ground near the base of some trees. He started to pull things out of his red leather pouch. A bedroll, a small tarp, and a pillow, all made from what appeared to be velvet leaves.

He made a small sleeping space and then moved on to an open area and proceeded to make a campfire. Once the fire was lit, he pulled a little cooking pot and some rations out of his pouch.

Crawl couldn't take it any longer, "How does all of that fit into that tiny little hip pouch?"

Rumtuskin looked up at Crawl and smiled, "It's a magic pouch. It will hold just about anything I put in it."

"What won't it hold?" Burble asked.

"What do you mean?" Rumtuskin asked.

"You said it will hold just about anything you put in it," Burble said. "What won't it hold?"

Rumtuskin looked down at the little pouch. "I actually don't know. I've never had anything that didn't fit into it. But I haven't really tried to put anything that remarkable into it."

"What is it made out of?" Crawl asked. "Everything else you have seems to be made from Burble's leaves."

"It was made by my mother," Rumtuskin said. "It's the pouch she used to gather her herbs in. The magic she used is magic that I am not talented in, but my father gave it to me after my mother died."

"Oh, I'm sorry about your mother," Burble said. "Has it been long?"

Rumtuskin suddenly looked very sad and shook his head. "It's been less than a year."

"Oh, I'm so sorry, Rumtuskin," Burble said. "Is that why you're gathering?"

Rumtuskin nodded. "My mother always said I should develop my magic. Tailor magic is a rare skill among the dwarves. Even among the gnomes. But I never was brave enough to pursue it."

"What did your father say about it?" Crawl asked.

"He was always against it," Rumtuskin said. "Until my mother died. Then he suddenly said I should follow my heart."

"What changed his mind?" Burble asked.

"My mother," Rumtuskin said. "My father took a lot of abuse from other dwarves about marrying my mother. But he followed his heart. When she died, he said he would never have chosen differently. It was then that he realized that I needed to follow my heart too. He gave me her gathering bag and told me to pursue learning my tailor magic. He gave me his blessing and sent me on my way."

"Wow," Burble said. "Is that when you found us.?"

"No," Rumtuskin shook his head. "I found another tailor magician in a village. He took me on as an apprentice, but after a few months, he had taught me all he knew."

"A few months?" Crawl said.

"Yes," Rumtuskin said. "He wasn't very good. But he was very nice. He taught me some basics and helped me get through some of my grief. And his wife was a wonderful cook."

Rumtuskin sat down in front of the fire and started putting his dinner together. He put his rations into the little pot and hung it over the fire with a stick and a hook.

"I would offer you both some, but I don't think we eat the same things," Rumtuskin said.

"The moss on the ground is plenty for me, but thank you," Burble said. "And Crawl is taken care of."

"I've read a lot about your kind," Rumtuskin said. "But you two were the first I had come across. And when I realized that Burble shed his leaves naturally, I just started following you."

"That's quite all right," Burble said. "You've been wonderful company. The only one I have to talk to is Crawl, and he's a grump."

"Hey," Crawl objected.

"Well, you are," Burble said.

"Well, I thank you for allowing me to accompany you," Rumtuskin said. "And I will gladly show you any of my tailor magics if you would like to watch."

"I still don't trust him," Crawl whispered.

"As for your King," Rumtuskin said. "I mean him no harm. And I will wait wherever you would like me to when you visit him."

"I think you should come with us," Burble said.

"What?" Crawl and Rumtuskin said in unison.

"I think you would be a wonderful liaison for the dwarves," Burble said. "King DaeMark is a kind man. Maybe you can help establish peace between your people and his."

"I can't speak for my people," Rumtuskin said. "They would never allow it."

"Well, then," Burble said. "You will come as our guest."

"We can't do that," Crawl whispered.

"Yes, we can," Burble said. "And we are."

"I accept your offer on one condition," Rumtuskin said. "If the King does not wish to have me there, I leave. I don't want to cause trouble."

"Agreed," Burble said. "But I guarantee you that the King will be happy to greet you as an honored guest."

"We'll see," Crawl grumbled.

***

Sometime, long after midnight, there was a rustling in the trees above the small camp. The fire was still burning, and it cast a soft glow across the sleeping figures and disappeared into the darkness.

Crawl awoke first and stared up into the shadowy branches of the trees against the night sky.

"Alert," Crawl yelled. "Alert! Wake up!"

Burble woke up quickly and Rumtuskin was already on his feet.

"What's the matter?" Rumtuskin asked.

"Drop bears!" Crawl said. "Be ready."

Rumtuskin pulled a small sword out of his pouch and waited for the inevitable attack. "Drop bears?"

"They hunt in small packs," Crawl warned.

"What do they eat?' Rumtuskin asked.

"Anything they can find," Burble answered.

Moments later, the first small fuzzy creature fell from the treetops. It was followed by a small shower of several more.

Burble used his branches to swat them away while Crawl and Rumtuskin put up a fight. After a short flurry of Crawl catching the leaping bears, Rumtuskin ran them through.

When the short battle was over, Rumtuskin squatted down next to one of the creatures and looked at it.

"They're really kind of cute," Rumtuskin said.

"I know," Burble said. "It's a shame to have to fight them."

"They eat dwarves as well as tree bark," Crawl reminded them.

Rumtuskin looked around at the small mass of fluffy bears. There were about a half dozen of them laying around their encampment. "Now what?"

"Your pouch," Burble cried.

Rumtuskin turned in the direction that Burble was stretching his branches.

Rumtuskin's pouch had been kicked to the side in the scuffle with the bears and had landed at the edge of the fire. One side of it was already ablaze.

"No," Rumtuskin raced towards the fire and pulled the pouch to safety and stomped the fire out. He stood over it and watched with tears in his eyes as the contents spilled out all over the ground in front of him. His camping supplies, his clothes, and his velvet cloth all laid on the ground next to the smoldering pouch.

"Is it all right?" Burble asked as he made his way over to Rumtuskin's side.

"No," the dwarf shook his head. "The magic is gone. It's just a pouch."

"Can you fix it?" Burble asked.

"No," Rumtuskin shook his head. "I don't know that kind of magic."

"I'm sorry," Burble said. "Can we help?"

Rumtuskin shook his head again, "I just need a moment."

"With the drop bears?" Burble asked.

"No," Rumtuskin shook his head. "Not with the drop bears."

Burble and Crawl gave Rumtuskin a few minutes alone. He sat by the fire with his mother's pouch and stared at the red leather. He ran his fingers over the runes that had been engraved in it by his mother's hands and then held it close to his chest.

After a few minutes, Crawl spoke up.

"I don't mean to rush you," Crawl said. "But scavengers will be along soon for the bears."

"It will be dawn soon," Rumtuskin agreed. "We should move."

Rumtuskin collected his things and made a small backpack out of his bedroll and some rope that he had stashed with his gear. When all his things were collected and tucked safely away, he hoisted the pack onto his shoulders and kicked out the fire.

"We should go," Rumtuskin said quietly.

***

Rumtuskin remained quiet for most of the journey. They finally hit the paths leading to the city of Shal Tahl. Burble moved slowly along the gravel, so progress was slow as they headed towards the Crystal Tower where the King lived.

"Over this hill, there is a large meadow, we can pick up speed there," Crawl said to Rumtuskin.

The dwarf nodded.

As they reached the peak of the hill, they stopped and stared at what they saw.

The town was being raided by soldiers, and there was chaos everywhere. People were running through the streets being chased by the enemy soldiers. Homes burned from fires set by the general's torches.

"What's happening?" Rumtuskin asked.

"Those soldiers are from Talask's army," Burble said.

"Who's?" Rumtuskin asked.

"The King's older brother," Crawl said. "He thinks the kingdom is rightfully his, but their father disowned him."

"For what?" Rumtuskin asked.

"For things like this," Burble said.

The King's army was filling the village. They started to battle Talask's soldiers.

"There's the King," Burble said.

"Where?" Rumtuskin was having trouble finding him in the crowd.

"There," Burble said. "With the family with the baby."

Rumtuskin looked and saw the King pulling a young couple out of harm's way. He pushed them in the direction of safety, and then turned to fight one of Talask's men.

The young man drew his sword and fought by the King's side.

His wife hesitated for a moment, and then hid the baby among a pile of baskets in front of a small shop. She then took a sword from a fallen man nearby and fought alongside her husband.

"We have to help," Rumtuskin said. "Look!"

Rumtuskin dropped his backpack and took off running through the meadow.

Burble and Crawl saw what the dwarf was pointing at.

One of the generals was heading through the town setting shops on fire and the basket shop was in his path.

Rumtuskin ran as fast as his legs could carry him and he made it to the basket shop in time to grab the basket that the baby was in. The general started to set fire to the basket stand and saw Rumtuskin with the child.

"Just where do you think you're going with a human child?" the general looked down at Rumtuskin and the baby.

Rumtuskin didn't say anything, he just picked up the basket with the child in it and adjusted her blanket. Her sweet face looked up at him as he covered her mouth and nose and tucked the pale pink fabric in around her face. He ignored the smoke in the air that was starting to choke him. He carefully put the basket over one shoulder and turned to run.

"That baby is mine," the general said. "Give it to me."

The general started after Rumtuskin but was stopped by the King's voice behind him.

"Talask!"

Rumtuskin stared wide eyed back at the general, who stopped and turned to look at the King.

"Little brother," he tossed the torch into the last of the baskets and pulled out his sword. "I've been waiting for this moment."

Rumtuskin seized the moment to take the baby and run.

***

Rumtuskin kept his eyes focused on the path towards the top of the hill. He tried not to jiggle the baby too much, but to no avail. She lay in the basket and cried as he ran with her in the basket back towards Burble and Crawl. His lungs burned with the effort and the sting of the smoke, but he made it to the top and laid the basket down under the safety of Burble's branches.

Rumtuskin checked on the baby and cooed to her softly to get her to stop crying. He scurried to his pack and pulled out a small rag, his water bag, and his sword.

"What are you going to do?" Crawl asked.

Rumtuskin quickly soaked the rag and gave the baby some water. He wiped her face with the cool rag and then picked up his sword.

"Take care of her," Rumtuskin said.

"What?" Crawl asked. "We're not babysitters."

"We will protect her with our lives," Burble said. "For the King."

Rumtuskin took off running down the hill again. He headed back towards the basket shop, in hopes of finding the baby's mother.

He saw her in the distance, battling with one of Talask's men. She was impressive with a sword and was holding her own quite well. But a second soldier spotted them and went over to join the fight.

Rumtuskin charged at the second soldier, with his small sword held out in front of him. He had never done battle with humans before, but he reminded himself that he had slain an owlephant in the forest, so he charged on. He didn't realize that he was screaming until the soldier turned.

He caught the soldier somewhat by surprise and as he swung around to see who was noisily attacking, Rumtuskin had time to hamstring him, his dwarven blade sharp enough to cut through the soldier's boots.

The man fell to the ground, screaming and Rumtuskin finished him.

He turned to the soldier who was battling with the baby's mother. It was too late. He watched as the baby's mother fell to the ground after the soldier removed his blade from her chest.

Before the soldier could turn around, Rumtuskin did the same attack on him as he had done on his friend. He pushed past the body of the soldier and ran to the baby's mother, who was laying on the ground, gasping for air.

"My baby," she whispered to him. "You have to find my baby."

"I did," Rumtuskin said to her. "She's safe."

The woman smiled weakly. "Thank you."

"Where is your husband?" he asked, looking around for the man who had been fighting at the King's side.

"He's dead," she shook her head. "He defended the King. He was so brave. The King is still alive because of him."

She looked proud for a moment.

"You have to take care of my daughter," she said. "Find her a home. We have no other family."

"I promise," Rumtuskin said.

He held her hand as she gasped for air.

"Her name is Shyeanna," she said. "Please, take care of her."

"I promise, it will be done," Rumtuskin said. "She will be safe."

The woman took her last gasping breath and closed her eyes.

For the first time on a battlefield, Rumtuskin knelt and took off his hat. He took the Dwarvish Time for the Dead in the middle of battle.

***

Talask had believed that his brother's soldiers were not in the city that day. He was wrong. It was a hard but short battle. Talask had underestimated the number of soldiers that would come to the town's aid during the attack.

Outnumbered by too large of a ratio, Talask had ordered his remaining soldiers to retreat. Once again, Talask suffered a loss at the hands of his younger brother. Which all but guaranteed that he would be back to fight for what he felt was rightfully his.

King DaeMark helped the townspeople put out the fires and directed the injured be taken to the Crystal Tower's infirmary.

Rumtuskin watched with awe as the King assisted his people. He was one of them, and they accepted him as one of them. There were very few formalities, and he seemed to know a lot of the townspeople by name.

DaeMark finished helping an injured man onto a stretcher and watched as two of his soldiers carried him off to the castle.

The King turned and saw Rumtuskin standing in the middle of the road, his Dwarven sword at his side.

DaeMark approached the dwarf.

"You fought bravely," DaeMark said. "Thank you."

"I was only trying to find the parents of the infant," Rumtuskin said.

"You know where she is?" DaeMark said. "Please, tell me."

"She's at the top of the hill leading into the town to the north," Rumtuskin said. "She's being watched over by some friends."

"Is she all right?" DaeMark asked.

"She's fine," Rumtuskin said. "I promised her mother I would find her a good home."

"She will stay with me," DaeMark said. "Her parents both died in battle by my side, defending me from my brother and his soldiers. She will be my daughter."

Rumtuskin stared at the King.

"Well, then," he gathered himself. "Let me go introduce you to your daughter."

Rumtuskin led the King towards the hill, but Burble and Crawl were already heading down, the basket snuggled up tightly to Burble's trunk by a cooing Crawl.

"Burble, is that you?" DaeMark asked, jogging towards the velvet tree.

"Yes, my King," Burble said. "We kept the baby safe for our friend, Rumtuskin."

DaeMark took the basket from Burble and stared down at the sleeping child.

"The three of you saved her life," DaeMark said. "I thank you."

"Her name is Shyeanna," Rumtuskin said.

DaeMark picked Shyeanna up out of the basket and held her in his arms.

"Hello, beautiful girl," he whispered. "When you wake up, you will be a princess."

                                    ***

       The day after the wounded were tended to, and
accommodations were found for those who had lost
homes, DaeMark asked Burble, Crawl, and Rumtuskin
to meet with him in the Crystal Tower.
       They met with him in the conservatory, which
was where Burble and Crawl spent a lot of their time
while in the city. Burble loved to soak his roots in the
spring water that flowed from underground into the
indoor greenhouse.
       Rumtuskin looked around at the huge glass
covered room. There was every kind of plant he could
imagine. The scent of the variety of flowers was
intoxicating. He had never really smelled flowers
growing indoors before. The scents were trapped in the
room and magnified by the sun. It was powerful.
       "Welcome, my friends," King DaeMark said as
he entered the room.
       "Your Majesty," Rumtuskin bowed to the
King.
       "No need for that," DaeMark said. "I don't
dwell on formalities. Especially with my friends."
       "I'm a friend?" Rumtuskin was amazed. "I
barely even know you. And I am a dwarf."
       "I know your character," DaeMark said. "I saw
you in battle. You are a man of honor. And even more
than that, you have a good heart. That is all that
matters to me."
       "He saw the baby in jeopardy, and he ran down
the hill and into battle with no thought for himself,"
Burble said proudly. "I am honored to call Rumtuskin
my friend."

"I am as well," the King said.

"I would like to offer the new princess a gift," Rumtuskin said.

He pulled a baby blanket out of his pack that was made from Burble's leaves. Rumtuskin had worked on it all night. He handed it to the King.

DaeMark ran the fabric through his fingers. "It's absolutely beautiful. I've never seen its equal."

"Thank you," Rumtuskin said.

"He made it from my leaves," Burble said proudly.

"Well, Burble," the King smiled. "You do make the most beautiful leaves of all of your kind."

Crawl stifled a small laugh.

"Thank you for the gift, Rumtuskin," DaeMark said. "The princess will love it."

Rumtuskin nodded and smiled.

"I owe the three of you a debt of gratitude," DaeMark said. "What can I do for you?"

"Nothing," Rumtuskin said. "I do not do battle with honor for a reward."

"I know what you can do," Burble said.

"Name it, old friend," DaeMark said. "And it's yours."

"Would you summon Cassandra here please?" Burble asked.

DaeMark gave Burble an inquisitive look but asked his guards at the door to do so.

A few minutes later, a gnomish woman entered the room. She was only slightly taller than Rumtuskin and wore a white apron over her pale blue dress. Her dark green hair was pulled into a braid that flowed down her back.

Her hair reminded Rumtuskin of his mother.

Rumtuskin brightened when he saw her and looked between Burble and Cassandra with interest.

"Here she is," DaeMark said. "What do you wish to ask her?"

Burble moved forward to greet the woman. "I don't know if you can help, but my friend Rumtuskin has a bag that was created by his mother. She was half gnome, and I was wondering if you knew a similar magic, so you could fix it?"

Rumtuskin gasped and looked at Cassandra.

"What kind of gnomish magic?" she asked.

Crawl produced the pouch and handed it out to Cassandra.

"Where did you get that?" Rumtuskin asked.

"You sleep soundly, my friend," Crawl said.

Cassandra looked it over. She held it in her hands and shut her eyes.

"Oh yes," she said. "I can feel the magic. I know it."

"You can fix it?" Rumtuskin was hopeful.

"I think so, give me a moment," she said.

Cassandra took the pouch over to the spring that Burble had been soaking in and submerged it into the clear spring water.

Rumtuskin gasped as he watched the water completely cover the red leather.

"It will be fine," she said. "Come and watch if you wish."

Rumtuskin and DaeMark both went over and watched over the girl's shoulder.

She sang softly in gnomish to the pouch, weaving her magic into the water.

The burned area on the pouch slowly restored itself, and the pouch started to glow. Her singing increased in rhythm and cadence slightly and she pulled the pouch out of the water.

Rumtuskin hadn't realized that he was holding his breath until he was watching her dry the pouch off with her apron.

She looked up and smiled at Rumtuskin and held the pouch out to him.

"It should be as good as new," she said.

"Thank you," Rumtuskin said.

He reached out to take the bag from her and they both stood there, their eyes locked, each holding the pouch for a moment.

"Your mother's magic was strong," she smiled. "I was able to keep what remained of her magic in it."

"My mother's magic is still there?" Rumtuskin finally took the pouch from her and ran his hand over it once again. This time it was whole and unblemished.

Cassandra nodded. "I used what was left of her magic and weaved in my own."

"Thank you," Rumtuskin said. "How can I ever repay you?"

Cassandra smiled, "Maybe I could make you dinner sometime?"

Rumtuskin blushed. "How would that be me repaying you?"

"I'm sure you'll think of something," Cassandra winked and turned to leave the room.

"Thank you, Cassie," DaeMark grinned as she walked past him.

Rumtuskin watched the girl go in awe.

"She's amazing," Rumtuskin whispered.

Crawl knocked Rumtuskin in the back of his hat.

"I'm sorry," Rumtuskin said, blushing.

"It's not a problem," DaeMark smiled. "She's a wonderful girl, you couldn't find better."

Rumtuskin ran his hands over his pouch once again. "I can't believe it's fixed."

His eyes welled with tears. "I will have to make her something amazing."

"I feel a cold coming on," Burble said. "You'll have your supplies in no time."

"I have one last favor to ask of the three of you," DaeMark said.

"Anything, old friend," Crawl answered.

"I've never raised a child," DaeMark said. "And I think it is only appropriate to ask the ones who rescued her to become her godparents."

Rumtuskin looked at the King in amazement.

"Yes, we would love to," Burble squealed.

"What?" said Crawl.

"You want a dwarf to be the godparent of a princess of Shal Tahl?" Rumtuskin whispered.

"I would love to have such a brave man as an example for my daughter," DaeMark said.

"I would," Rumtuskin stammered. "Yes, I accept."

"That leaves you, Crawl," DaeMark looked at the ivy.

"She's a beautiful child," Crawl said. "I don't know what a symbiote ivy would do for her upbringing, but I humbly accept."

"Then it's settled," DaeMark said. "Rumtuskin, if you would do us the honor of staying with us here in the Crystal Tower, I will have a room set up for you. Just tell me what you need."

"Just a bed and a chair, sir," Rumtuskin said. "I need a place to sleep and to continue to learn my magic."

"I'm sure we can do better than that," DaeMark said. "And don't call me sir. You are my child's godfather, DaeMark will do."

"Yes, sir," Rumtuskin said. "I mean DaeMark."

"You are still learning your tailor magic?" DaeMark asked.

"Yes," Rumtuskin nodded. "I had a teacher, but he didn't know more than basics."

"We have a wonderful tailor here in the Tower," DaeMark said. "And if I'm not mistaken, he's been talking about retiring if he could find an apprentice."

"You mean?" Rumtuskin stammered. "He's here in the castle?"

DaeMark nodded. "I could speak to him for you."

"Yes, please," Rumtuskin nodded happily. "This is all like a dream."

DaeMark laughed. "Not quite. And we must always be ready for Talask's return. Part of the royal tailor's duties is also helping with my soldier's armor."

"That won't be a problem," Rumtuskin said. "I would love to learn whatever he has to teach."

REALITY FAILS
A JOSHUA FAHLSTROM SHORT STORY
JUDY LUNSFORD

Reality Fails

This is the first short story in a series of short stories about Joshua Fahlstrom and his adventures in closing rifts in reality that lead to other random dimensions. It is an urban fantasy and has started in short stories.
As of March 2021, there are three stories available with a fourth on the way.

The reality in the women's restroom in the bookstore on 3rd St was failing.

This wasn't a completely uncommon occurrence for a bookstore. In fact, I was on a first name basis with the manager. It was just unfortunate that it was in the bathroom this time, but that's where some people go to read.

I hung up my phone and gathered my supplies.

Bookstores were a more difficult beast because of the books. Libraries were worse. But I actually didn't mind. This was my job and I rather liked it.

My name is Joshua Fahlstrom, and I am a thaumaturge.

That means magician or wizard or mage, or whatever name someone wants to give it. I like the name thaumaturge because it doesn't have the fantasy book connotations that some of the other titles do. Especially since fantasy books tend to be one of my biggest problems. But they bring me clients, so I can't bad mouth them too much.

When I got to the bookstore, Greg, the owner and manager, met me at the door. He was tall and lean and wore really thick glasses. His pants were always about an inch too short and he always wore funny and colorful socks of various kinds. Today's socks were bright sky blue with little sushi rolls all over them.

"Josh, you gotta come see this," he grabbed me by the arm and dragged me to the back of the store.

He led me to the ladies' room at the back corner of the store. He had already put an out of order sign on the door and put a "knock first" sign on the men's room.

He unlocked the door with a key and led me inside.

Greg locked the door behind us.

It was a single toilet restroom, one with no stalls, but with plenty of space for the sink and, curiously, a plush red velvet chaise lounge in the corner.

"Do people really use that in here?" I pointed at the chaise.

"I have no idea," Greg said. "I don't come in here with them."

"So, where's the problem?" I asked.

"Just wait," Greg said.

My nose was already getting assaulted by the rose scented potpourri that was on a small shelf above the sink. It was potent. And not a good idea in a bookstore.

"You know the potpourri is part of the problem, right?" I asked.

"What do you mean?" Greg looked at the pretty little glass bowl filled with dried flowers and other bits.

"The roses attract fae," I said. "I'm betting you're having a fairy problem in here, no?"

"I don't know if it's fae," Greg looked at me and then back at the bowl. "My wife put it there, she'll kill me if I take it down."

"Not if an angry faerie gets to you first," I said.

The light in the ceiling flickered.

"Okay, here it comes," Greg pointed to the wall over the toilet. "Just watch."

The wall suddenly looked like it was crumbling away, and a dark void could be seen behind it.

There was a gust of wind sucking the air inward, through the void. It was an angry one. Probably because it was stuck in a bathroom.

"I bet the woman reading there was in for a fright," I tried not to laugh. This was Greg's livelihood we were dealing with.

"She ran out the door without even pulling her pants up," Greg said. "She screamed the whole way through the store and out the door."

I bit my lip to keep from laughing. Because in reality, it wasn't funny. That woman will probably need therapy for years.

"She's lucky she didn't get sucked through into the void," I said.

Greg shook his head, "I don't need any more bad publicity. This is the second time this month."

"Maybe you should have a no books allowed in the bathroom rule," I said.

"I do," Greg objected. "Nobody follows it."

"Okay, down to business," I said. "Do we know what book she was reading?"

"No," Greg shook his head. "She took it with her as she ran out."

I shook my head as I put my leather satchel down on the chaise. "That makes it more difficult."

"Well, it's obviously something sci-fi, right?" Greg pointed to the void.

"Maybe," I said. "Maybe not. Stay back."

I took a few steps closer to see if I could get a look out the hole. But before I could get close enough, it abruptly closed.

"How long are the intervals between it opening?" I asked.

"They're getting shorter each time," Greg said. "It's at about three minutes now."

"Okay," I said. "Then we wait."

We stood there awkwardly to wait for the void to open again.

"How versed are you on sci-fi?" I asked.

"It's one of my favorite genres," Greg said.

"So, if you got close enough, could you maybe tell what book we're dealing with?" I asked. "Even if it's only narrowed down to a series, that would be helpful."

"Are you kidding me?" Greg's eyes were wide. "I'm not going any closer to that thing than I am now."

I sighed. I didn't have much time to read, so I was going to be no help at identifying what we were dealing with.

I really needed Greg to buck up and help.

"Would you feel better about it if I got some rope and anchored you down, so you can't get lost?" I asked.

"Not if some creature lops my head off when I stick it through the hole," Greg said.

He was never a big help in these situations. He was one of those who only read about heroes but had no desire to become one.

"Fine," I said. "I'll do it. If I describe what I see, will you be able to identify the book?"

"Maybe," Greg said.

"Good enough," I sighed.

The lights flickered once again, right on time.

The void opened up and the suction started to pull on the room even harder this time.

I inched my way up to the void and had to rest a foot on the back of the toilet seat in order to get close enough to see through the hole.

All I could see was outer space. Once my head was actually through the hole, there was no wind, no suction, just quiet. It was peaceful.

I saw an odd-looking ship far below me. I described it to Greg.

There was no answer from him.

I pulled my head back inside and looked at him expectantly.

"Well?" he asked.

"Couldn't you hear me?" I asked.

"No," Greg looked genuinely surprised that I thought I had spoken. "I couldn't hear a thing."

I described the ship to him. Again.

His eyes grew wide.

"We have to shut it," he said. "I think I know what ship that is, and we have to shut it, now."

"Okay," I said. "Do we think anything has come through?"

"I really hope not," he said. "But we have to shut it and worry about that later."

"What book is it?" I asked.

He told me. My eyes widened. I had never read the book, but I had seen the movie. And all of the sequels. We needed to shut that void.

It wasn't a straight up sci-fi, it was a horror movie. I mean book.

Whatever, we had to shut it before something our world couldn't handle came crawling through that hole.

I turned to get my supplies, but I heard an awful noise behind me.

That meant it was at the void.

I looked back at the hole and a huge monster was trying to rip the hole bigger. It wasn't the creature I was expecting. It was a whole lot bigger and scarier than the one I saw in the movie.

"Are you sure you have the right book?" I yelled to Greg over the screeching noise that the monster was making.

There was no answer because Greg had left the restroom.

I went back to my bag and started pulling supplies out. Anything I thought might be useful for forcing an alien monster back through a reality collapsing void and back into the book it came from.

It would help immensely to know what story this creature actually came from, but it was too late for that now. I had to focus on generalities instead of specifics.

The goal was to close the void. For good.

I pulled out the supplies I needed for closing just an average void. One where reality was collapsing and there was nothing specific coming through the wall at me with sharp claws and teeth.

I turned back to the creature. I was dismayed to see that three of its arms were already through the hole and reaching out for me. I'm not sure how many more arms the creature had, and I had no desire to find out.

As I dodged a clawed hand, I dropped a key ingredient and the vial smashed on the floor, sending broken glass and a red dust all over the floor.

I tried to scoop up some of the dust, but the creature grabbed the collar of my jacket with just the tip of an outstretched claw and started to pull me towards it and away from the red dust on the floor.

I could feel its other claws scratching at me, coming closer to ripping out my ribcage with every swipe.

There was a horrible crunching sound and the creature released me with a horrifying scream.

I looked up to see that the void had closed on the creature, holding it firmly in place.

I had three minutes.

Three minutes to prep my spell and get ready to force the creature back through the void when it opened again, then shut the void for good.

I readied my ingredients, all the while avoiding the claws that were once again reaching out for me.

The creature was still alive and still hungry, apparently.

I readied the spell as quickly as I could and then looked for something, anything, that could force the creature back through the hole when it opened again.

Greg opened the door the tiniest bit and peeked in to see how I was doing.

I grabbed him by the shoulder and dragged him inside.

"I need your help," I said.

"That's not the right creature," he said.

"I know," I said. "It doesn't matter. We need to force it back when the void opens."

He looked at me in horror. "How?"

"With this," I grabbed my satchel and threw it on the floor and dragged the chaise into position. "We hit it with the chaise to force it back. Then I throw this through after it."

I held up a glass beaker where I had put all of the spell ingredients that I needed.

"That's not going to work," he said.

"You have twenty seconds to come up with a better plan," I said.

He stared at me and then grabbed the back end of the chaise.

"Good man," I said.

We lifted the chaise onto our shoulders and as the lights flickered, I started our countdown.

"Three, two, one," I said. "Push."

As the void released the creature, we smashed it in the face with the chaise.

The creature held on with its claws to the tile above the toilet and its head was forced back by the surprise blow to the head.

I tossed the beaker through the hole and screamed, "Clusus."

The void slammed shut and only the fingers of the creature were left on our side.

The fingers fell to the floor and a bluish green ooze dripped down the wall from where they fell.

We both stood there, breathing heavily, and stared at the fingers on the floor.

"I don't want to touch those," Greg said.

I glared at him and went to my satchel. I pulled out another glass vile, a big one, and scooped the fingers into it. I magically sealed the bottle shut and put it back into my bag.

Greg stared at the wall. Quite a few tiles had been ripped off the wall and were laying on the floor in pieces.

"I guess the ladies' room will be out of order for a little while longer," I said.

Greg sighed. "My brother-in-law is a contractor," he said. "I guess I'll just owe him another favor.

I nodded. I grabbed a rag from my supplies and mopped up the alien creature's blood.

"Be careful," Greg said.

"It's not acid, if that's what you're worried about," I said.

"It could be anything," Greg said. "Don't touch it."

I put the rag into yet another glass container and tucked it down in my bag.

"Don't worry," I said. "I have a ritual that will send all of the remains back to the book it came from. I just don't have the right supplies on me."

Greg nodded.

He looked back at the wall where the void had been and then over at the potpourri.

"And you were worried about faeries, huh?" he chuckled.

"Yeah," I laughed. "This one was much easier than faeries."

Greg's eyes widened and he grabbed the bowl of potpourri.

"I'd rather have my wife kill me than something else," Greg said.

I just laughed as he ran out the door to dispose of the rancid flowers.

In reality, faeries were much easier to deal with than alien creatures. I just didn't want to come back and work in a bathroom again.

Judy Lunsford
Shandoah
A Fire Lily short story

Shandoah

Shandoah *is a short story I wrote to introduce the **Fire Lily** trilogy. As of March 2021, the trilogy is slated to be released in April, July, and October of 2021. The trilogy is finished, just waiting to be released. Shandoah got her own short story because she was one of my favorite characters and never got highlighted the way she deserved to be. Sometimes it sucks being a secondary character.*

Shandoah ran through the forest, smacking the trees who were sleeping, just to wake them up. She giggled as she ran and savored the smells of spring as they were stirred up by her feet kicking up the moss and soil.

Shandoah loved spring. Most dryads did, although she couldn't understand how they possibly could if they were still asleep. In the spring, Shandoah couldn't contain her joy, hence the running and the giggling.

She could hear the angry shouts of the older dryad behind her, rousing from their hibernation. She ignored them and kept running.

Her bare feet slapped against the ground, intentionally splashing through the puddles left behind by a warm spring rain that she had enjoyed earlier that morning. Her toes squished in the cold mud and she loved the sound it made.

When she reached the clearing, she finally stopped. The sun was shining down through the gray clouds that were being blown away by the breeze. She took in the warmth and watched as the birds started to come out from their shelters to join her in the sunlight.

She spread her arms wide and soaked in spring. She relished the fact that the long winter was over and that, once again, sleep would be reserved only for night.

"Shandoah, come here," a loud voice said from behind her.

Shandoah cringed and she turned slowly to face the direction of the voice she knew all too well.

"Grandfather," she said sheepishly. Shandoah realized that in her haste, she must have slapped him as well.

"What is the meaning of your disturbance?" he demanded.

Her grandfather was standing in the clearing, also in his elven form. Shandoah could remember when they got along. When he spent more time playing with her and telling her stories while she sat on his knee, rather than lecturing her and yelling at her loud enough to scatter the birds back into the treetops.

"It's spring," Shandoah couldn't hide the glee from her voice.

"Yes, it is spring," her grandfather said, as he smoothed out his long gray beard. "But that is no excuse for your behavior."

"I'm so sorry," she looked down at her feet and noticed tiny little flowers were already peeking their way up through the grass. "I just couldn't contain myself."

"Well, try," her grandfather snapped. "You've awoken the whole tribe with your antics."

"Good," Shandoah said before she could bite her tongue.

She knew it was a mistake as soon as she said it.

"Good?" her grandfather took a step towards her. "You think your disgraceful behavior is acceptable?"

Shandoah felt a surge of bravery, or possibly stupidity, and said, "Yes! It's spring! Everyone should be awake."

Her grandfather took a breath to respond, but before he could, Shandoah let out a screech and then with a whooping yell and turned on her heel to run once again.

She hollered the whole way through the clearing and almost slipped in the mud as she splashed through another puddle that was a little deeper than she expected.

When she was sure that she had run far enough, she looked back through the maple and elm trees to make sure her grandfather hadn't followed her. She knew he wouldn't. He was too dignified to run. They all were, and that made her angry all of a sudden.

She looked around at the trees that were already showing their vividly green leaves. The sun was shining, and it was a wonderfully warm morning. She couldn't understand how they could possibly still sleep.

She watched the birds cheerfully singing and flitting from branch to branch overhead. She caught sight of one of her favorites, a gorgeous robin, as it gathered materials from the ground. She watched in wonder as it flew up to where he and his mate were furiously building their nest.

"They're missing it," she whispered. "They're missing all of this."

"Of course they are," a tiny voice said from behind her.

Shandoah wasn't expecting a response. She whipped around to see a forest sprite hovering in the air nearby. The sprite was wearing the magenta petals of a fireweed as a dress. Shandoah could smell the petals from where she was standing, so the flowers were fresh.

"I love your new dress," Shandoah said to her.

The forest sprite touched the petals and giggled, "Thank you, I made it this morning."

"What's your name?" Shandoah asked.

"Sheyla," the forest sprite said. "What's yours?"

Shandoah," she answered.

"That's an interesting name," Shayla said.

"My mother is an interesting dryad," Shandoah said.

"Is that so?" Sheyla said. "I will have to meet her sometime. I like interesting creatures."

Shandoah was distracted by another robin, flitting around on the ground nearby.

"Where are the other dryads?" Shayla asked.

"They are still working on waking up from hibernation."

"Then why are you so awake?" Shayla asked.

Shandoah shrugged, "I seem to have more energy than most dryads."

"Oh lovely," Shayla said, and she clapped her hands together with glee.

"What's lovely?" Shandoah asked.

"You're an interesting creature yourself," the sprite said.

"I don't know about that," Shandoah answered. "I seem to always be getting into trouble because of my energy."

Shayla smiled, "Exactly."

Shandoah shuffled her feet in the fresh dew on the grass at her feet.

"I was exploring the forest to see who else is awake," Shandoah said. "Would you like to join me?"

"Absolutely!" the sprite squealed. "I saw some of the most beautiful flowers over in a meadow, deeper in the forest. Would you like to see?"

"Yes," Shandoah said. "Lead the way."

The sprite turned and flew off ahead of Shandoah. She knew that sprites were creatures that were not to be trusted, but she was aching for adventure. She didn't see the harm in allowing a sprite to show her some early spring flowers in a meadow.

Shandoah followed her new friend. Sprites were surprisingly fast and Shandoah had to run as fast as she could to keep up.

The forest flashed by her in a blur as she kept her eyes fixed on the sprite and her little magenta dress as she darted through the trees. They went deeper and deeper into the forest, until they were in an area that even Shandoah was unfamiliar with.

When they reached the meadow, Shayla stopped so suddenly that Shandoah raced right past the sprite before she could will her feet to stop.

She skidded to a halt with a yelp and slid in the wet grass for another few feet before her motion finally ceased.

It was too late.

Shandoah slammed right into an ancient tree, rattling its branches almost as much as it rattled the teeth in her head.

The impact knocked the wind out of Shandoah. As she staggered backwards, gasping for air, she felt as if some of her magic had been knocked out of her as well.

"Are you all right?" Shayla asked.

"Stay quiet," Shandoah said. "Maybe it didn't wake him."

Shandoah's heart filled with dread and fear as she recognized the tree. It was one of the ancient ones. But worse than that, it was petrified.

Punished.

Imprisoned.

There was only one tree in the ancient forest that was petrified.

Anyon. He was a rogue of the ancients. He was petrified for crimes that were so old, Shandoah couldn't remember them. But she knew they had something to do with humans.

He hated them. Anyon wanted to eradicate them.

Dryads had no love for humans, but they didn't wish them harm either. They only wanted to live in peace, hidden away from human eyes.

But Anyon had tried to create dissent. He wanted a war. Shandoah racked her brain for what she had been taught about him. She remembered blood.

He had killed humans that wandered into the forest.

So, he had been petrified. His prison was hidden deep in the forest, where it was forbidden for dryads to tread.

Where Shandoah was forbidden to be.

This was a punishable offence.

"We have to leave," Shandoah whispered.

"No, wait," Shayla squealed. "You have to watch."

"Watch what?' Shandoah asked.

That's when Shandoah noticed the robin.

Her beloved favorite of the birds.

There was one at the base of Anyon. Dead. Its neck had been broken and cut, the bird's blood seeping into Anyon's roots. There was a circle of flowers from the meadow surrounding the base of the tree.

Shandoah looked at the sprite in horror.

"You're trying to wake him up," Shandoah said.

She spoke in a normal voice this time. Her whisper was lost somewhere in her shock and fear.

"I only needed one last ingredient," Shayla giggled. "The touch of a dryad."

Shandoah gasped.

She had been part of the spell. Shayla had lured her here on purpose.

"You used me," Shandoah said. "To wake him up?"

"We need him," Shayla said. "Don't you see? Too many humans have been encroaching into our forest. We need him."

"No," Shandoah said. "No, we don't."

Anyon's branches started to shake.

"I have to go," Shandoah turned and stumbled over her own feet trying to get out of the clearing.

"Wait," Shayla called out to her. "We still need you to finish the spell."

Shandoah was off and running again.

This time it was not fueled by the joy of spring. Her running was fueled by fear and horror. And the need to tell the others what she had done.

She would be punished. She knew this.

But her grandfather needed to know that Anyon was free.

Her grandfather would be the first one Anyon came after. He was the leader of the dryads and would have to be done away with in order for Anyon to make any headway with leading the dryads to war.

She had to tell him. Now.

Shandoah ran as fast as her legs could carry her through the forest.

When she finally arrived back at her grove, a few more of the dryads had awakened. Some were still in their tree form, but many were in their elven form.

"Grandfather," Shandoah cried. "Grandfather, I need to speak with you."

Her grandfather turned and looked at her. His long gray beard swished in the breeze as he turned.

"Anyon," she said between breaths. "He's awake."

The other dryads gasped in horror. The forest went completely silent. All eyes were on Shandoah as she tried to catch her breath.

"What do you mean, he's awake?" her grandfather asked. "How?"

"A forest sprite, she cast a spell," Shandoah said. She was aware that all the dryads were listening to her now. But she didn't care. They had to know.

"She would need the touch of a dryad to wake him," her grandfather said.

Shandoah could feel all the eyes of the dryads on her now. She looked around and saw that most were now awake, and she felt their eyes boring into her. She could feel their eyes as if they were tearing right through to her soul.

"She tricked me," was all Shandoah could manage.

Her grandfather sighed and looked at the ground.

Shandoah could hear the murmurs starting among the other dryads.

It was the first day of spring and Shandoah, the troublemaker, had already brought ruin upon them all.

"There's still another part of the spell that must be completed," her grandfather said.

"How do we know the sprite hasn't done it already?' Shandoah asked.

"Because you're still alive," her grandfather said.

Shandoah stared at her grandfather wide-eyed. "He has to kill me?"

Her grandfather nodded gravely. "Only the elders can break the spell without blood."

"So, what do we do now?" Shandoah asked.

"You must leave," her grandfather said.

"Leave?" Shandoah stared at her grandfather in disbelief. "For how long?"

"Forever," her grandfather said. "You have broken dryad law by releasing a petrified without permission."

"But I didn't mean to," Shandoah started.

"It doesn't matter," her grandfather said. "He is bound to the forest and cannot leave its boundaries until he takes your blood. You must leave, so that we may fix your blunder. But you are banished because you broke dryad law by releasing him, unintentional or not."

"But grandfather," Shandoah could feel the sting of tears in her eyes. "Where would I go?"

He shook his head sadly, "That is for you to decide."

Shandoah felt like the wind was knocked out of her again as her grandfather and the other dryads turned their backs on her and disappeared into the forest.

She was left, standing alone in the empty grove, with no other dryads except her mother.

Shandoah couldn't bring her eyes up to meet her mother's eyes. She couldn't stand to see the disappointment that she knew was there.

"My sweet child," her mother whispered.

Shandoah still couldn't meet her eyes, so her mother cupped Shandoah's chin and lifted her face towards her own. Her mother's hands were rough, like the bark of a tree, but they felt like the only bit of happiness that was left for Shandoah to hold on to. Her mother had stayed. She was the only one who had not turned her back on Shandoah.

"My child," her mother said softly. "Go to the swamps to the south. I have a friend there."

"A friend?" Shandoah couldn't remember her mother ever leaving the forest.

"When I was young, I was full of energy, like you," her mother said. Her hand slid down and took Shandoah's hand in hers. "You get your exuberance from me."

Shandoah managed a half-laugh. She had always wished to be like her mother.

"I ran away for a time when I was young," her mother said.

"You?" Shandoah gasped.

"Yes," her mother nodded. "Your grandfather was even stricter with me, if you can believe it."

Shandoah nodded. She could believe it. Being his daughter had to have higher expectations than being his granddaughter.

"Go find Arrose," her mother said. "She is a water elemental and the queen of the swamps. She will protect you and give you shelter. There are many runaways that find refuge there."

"A water elemental?" Shandoah had heard rumors of the elementals. None of them were good.

"She has a good heart," her mother said. "She takes in those that need homes. The swamp is a refuge."

Shandoah nodded. "I'll find her."

"Tell her you are my daughter," her mother said. "She'll understand."

"You're staying?" Shandoah's eyes filled with tears.

"I have to," her mother said. "It will be me that is needed to fix the spell that has been broken."

"But you'll be all right?" Shandoah asked.

Her mother nodded, choking back tears. "And so will you."

Shandoah threw her arms around her mother. "I'm so sorry."

"I know," her mother said. "Now go. Find Arrose."

Her mother let go of her and took a step back.

Shandoah took one last look at her mother and gave her a weak smile. "I love you."

"I love you too," her mother said. And then she turned her back on Shandoah and disappeared into the forest.

Shandoah choked back the tears once again. The first day of spring had already been forgotten. She had to find Arrose. A water elemental was now her only hope.

Shandoah turned to the south and started to run.

A Fairy Short Story
Moon Songs
Judy Lunsford

Moon Songs

*This one is not technically a part of a series as much as it was the story that inspired a series. This short story is about the garden that is part of the setting of **Moonlight Magic**.*

I fell in love with the garden and the characters, so it is now in the process of becoming a series. I don't know how many books will be in the series, but this current day magical fantasy is definitely in the works as of March 2021.

Once upon a darkness, there lived a goth girl. She bought a huge Victorian house right next to an old cemetery. She loved the view of the crumbling headstones peeking out of the unkempt grass.

She also loved to work in her garden. But she wanted her garden to be very special. One where the flowers would only bloom at night.

She set about placing old cast iron cauldrons along the edge of the porch and used them for pots for some of her flowers across the front of her house. She had a wrought iron fence that surrounded the yard in sharp spikes that the flowers could climb when they grew large enough.

She planted all sorts of plants and flowers around the yard, most of which would bloom in white and glow ghostly in the moonlight.

She also put up a bat house in the corner of the yard, hoping that a sweet night rodent would take up residence and eat any bugs that may invade her precious garden.

One night, shortly after she had finished working in the garden, the moon was full and shone down on her beautiful yard. The white flowers yawned and stretched and came to life as they soaked in the moonlight.

Annabel Lee, the girl's black cat, was lounging on the porch on the lookout for anything that might strike her fancy. She swished her tail as the flowers woke, and she crouched down on the wooden bench in front of the dark window to watch the garden come to life.

The Nottingham Catchflies stretched their fragrant blooms towards the sky and flitting moths seemed to come from nowhere to flock to the heavy fragrance that filled the air.

Elvira, a small bat who had just moved into the bat house that stood high in the yard, poked her head out of the hole and watched the moths dance above the Nottinghams. She swooped down low over the flowers and hunted to her heart's delight.

Annabel Lee watched with interest as Elvira danced and swooped in the air above the waking flowers.

The Moon Flowers stretched tall to reach for their namesake. They gazed at the sky and soaked in the light of the full moon and the twinkling stars.

While the flowers were enjoying the night air, they suddenly stopped when they heard something from deep in the cemetery.

Annabel Lee crouched low and looked through the fence towards the headstones whose silhouettes towered in the darkness.

Elvira swooped back to her new bat house and waited until she could identify the noise.

When all was quiet in the garden, they heard it again. A wailing cry coming from the darkness of the cemetery.

Annabel Lee sniffed the air and crept closer to the fence that divided the yard from the cemetery. She looked through the iron bars, but all she could see were the dark shapes of the headstones and the dark shapes of the weeping willows drooping their leaves over the pond in the center of the grass. The earthy scent mixed with the fragrance of the Nottinghams, but nothing else seemed out of the ordinary.

The Moon Flowers stretched to their full height and strained to listen in the quiet still air.

A wailing cry shattered the silence of the darkness in the cemetery again.

Annabel Lee looked out over her new flower friends, who seemed to understand the cries, but since cats don't speak flower, Annabel Lee had to wait and watch to see what would happen.

The cries continued all night, and the worried flowers in the garden hushed themselves in the fading moonlight. As dawn rose, the flowers all curled up and went to sleep for the daylight hours, but still worried among themselves about the wailing cries.

The following evening, as the day flowers across the street started to curl up to sleep for the night, some of the early rising night blooms heard the whispers among the day flowers.

"They are the voices of the dead," the day flowers whispered to one another. "Crying out in the night."

The Moon Flowers and the Nottinghams looked at one another in their beds and wondered if the voices would come again tonight.

As the rising moon fully woke them from their slumber, the Moon Flowers stretched their stems and reached towards the stars in the sky.

Annabel Lee once again made her way to the bench on the porch and nestled herself on the dark cushions and peeked through the potted Night-Blooming Jasmine that sprung out of the cauldrons. As she breathed in the sweet scent, Annabel Lee set her eyes on the cemetery. Through the fence, she hoped to catch a glimpse of whatever had made the haunting cries from the night before.

In the darkness, the cries could be heard through the still scented air. The night flowers listened, to see if they could make out what was being said.

Elvira flew off and into the cemetery, to see if she could find the source. The flowers waited with anticipation for their winged friend to come back with any news.

The wind began to whisper through the weeping willows and carried the cries across the grass and into the flowerbeds.

Elvira flew back overhead, and dropped a lone, withered daisy onto the porch steps, before flying back to her new house.

The night flowers peered expectantly at the daisy, who gasped and lay wilted on the step.

"What happened?" the Moon Flowers whispered.

The daisy lifted her head, looking at the flowers of the night. "We're scared."

All of the night flowers crouched and huddled together. "Of what?" they wondered and whispered.

The daisy blinked back her tears. "People cut us and leave us to die on the headstones and in the grass," she whispered. "We're scared of the dark."

The night flowers were appalled at the thought. "Why would they do this?"

"It's just what people do," the daisy whispered. "They do it to honor their dead. We sacrifice ourselves to pay honor to them. But it's so dark."

The Moon Flowers felt such compassion for the dying daisy, they started to sing softly, to comfort her from her fear of the night.

"That's nice," the daisy whispered. "If only my friends could hear."

So, the Nottinghams and the Jasmine joined in the chorus, raising their voices to the moon, hoping that the flowers that lay scared in the old cemetery, on all of the graves would hear their song and not be afraid of the night.

The daisy lay silently on the porch step, having breathed her last. But in her honor, the night blooming flowers sang beautiful songs of comfort to her friends that lay dying in the cemetery. They sang to them every night. As new flowers arrived to the cemetery daily, the night blooming flowers sang their songs to each one of them that passed away among the headstones.

Every night, Annabel Lee and Elvira came out to listen to the beautiful music that drifted along the wind mixed with the enchanting fragrance of the blooms.

And never again were there frightened cries in the night coming from the cemetery.

AERIS AWAKENS
JUDY LUNSFORD

Aeris Awakens

*This story was inspired by my older brother, who passed away in February of 2018. I enjoyed writing the story so much, I decided to keep it going through a short story trilogy entitled **The Wild Hunt**. It is a complete short story trilogy dedicated to my brother, Eric.*

Elijah muttered to himself as he slammed his shovel into the loosely packed snow over and over again.

He hated snow. The white featureless landscape it created. The frigid cold that made his fingers hurt, even through the warm black gloves his mom had sent him last Christmas.

He missed living where there was no snow in the winter. Where it was warmer and there was no shoveling every morning for months.

He shoveled pile after pile out of the driveway. His back had started to hurt and his arms already ached after only a few minutes. He scanned the driveway and the distance to the street.

Laziness won out and he gave up. He'd rather walk to work than continue shoveling. Elijah convinced himself that it wasn't that far.

He tossed the shovel back into the garage where it landed in the corner with a satisfying clang and fell to the floor, taking a rake and a broom with it. The clatter was loud and it probably could be heard by the neighbors. He didn't care. It was his garage. He could do what he wanted.

He stomped the snow off himself and went back inside to change into work clothes and dry boots.

Eli stood at his closet and looked at the contents. He grabbed the blue collared polo shirt required for his job and pulled it on. He kept his work shirts next to his cosplay garb. Next to what he'd rather be wearing.

The green leather armor hung unfinished in the closet and made him drift off into another world for a moment. A world where he was a hunter. A warrior. An elf ranger that had adventures and made his own decisions. Not someone who had to work in an electronics store to pay his half of the rent on a crappy apartment in a small tourist town.

Eli finished dressing and headed outside. Back into the frigid cold and the blinding white snow.

He trudged through the snow to work. He trudged through his day at the retail electronics store where he catered to snotty entitled tourists who had lost their phone chargers and headphones. His mind wandered throughout the day back to what he wished he could be. A warrior, free to roam the countryside. Saving village people from monsters and maidens from villains.

At the end of the day, he set back out into the freezing cold to trudge his way back home. Just so he could do it all again tomorrow.

He decided to take a shortcut through the woods that led to a clearing behind his apartment building. The risk of running into a bear was low this time of year. But he could let his mind wander again, to the life he wished he had.

He listened to the crunch of the snow beneath his boots with each step and breathed in the smell of the snow. People had argued with him that snow was just frozen water, and it didn't have a scent and that what he was smelling was a lack of smells, dampened by the snow itself.

But Eli disagreed. It smelled like calm.

The one time he liked the snow was at night. When it was quiet. When he didn't have to go to work. When he could enjoy the fact that he didn't have to be anywhere or do anything.

He crunched along in the moonlight, thinking about the fact that all he had to do tonight was make some dinner and play video games for the rest of the night. The only place he could live his dream.

He had leftover pizza waiting for him in the fridge and a scheduled game online with his friends. His 80th level character was waiting, patiently, for him to come back. His idea of a perfect evening.

As he went deeper into the woods, he saw something flicker past in his peripheral vision.

He turned to see a shadow ducking behind some trees a bit in the distance.

"Hello?" he stopped and called out to the shadow.

Everything stayed quiet. Almost too quiet. Eli couldn't remember the forest ever being so still before, even on a winter night.

"Is someone there?" Eli took a few steps toward the direction he thought the shadow had gone.

There was a clearing in the treetops, just large enough so he could see past the tall pines and view the sky above him. He looked up into the full moonlight and saw a large group of creatures running through the sky. Some looked like they could be men, others definitely weren't. It was an enormous and noisy charge that filled the sky and momentarily blocked out the moonlight. They raced across the view allowed by the treetops and out of sight. Eli could still hear the faint yelling of the charge ringing in his ears and trailing off into the distance.

He heard a twig crack in the trees and turned his head to see a form taking advantage of his lack of attention and making a run for it.

"Stop," Eli called out. "Wait."

Eli started through the snow and followed the shadowy figure through the forest.

Eli knew the forest well and took a turn to cut the shadowy figure off before it could escape deeper into the woods.

The trees flashed by as Eli closed in on his prey.

He grew close enough to reach out and grab the tunic of the person he was pursuing.

"Stop," Eli shouted.

His fingers caught in the rough fabric just enough to pull the man off balance and both of them went tumbling through the cold, wet snow.

The figure recovered quickly and tried to scramble off, but Eli recovered also and grabbed the shadowy figure by the foot.

"Stop," Eli said. "I'm not going to hurt you."

The figure whipped around and faced Eli in the moonlight.

"But I may just hurt you," it hissed.

Eli gasped as he saw the creature for the first time. It definitely wasn't human.

He had deep blue, almost purplish skin and his eyes glowed yellow in the darkness. He was wispy thin and lanky and extremely tall.

They both scrambled to their feet and Eli stood in front of the creature, who towered at least a full head taller than Eli. He had long black hair that was in thin braids that reached all the way to his waist.

The creature was wearing black leather armor that made him look like a shadow, even in the full moonlight.

"Nice armor," Eli whispered.

The creature pulled a sword from beneath his dark cape and placed it under Eli's chin before Eli had a chance to move.

"Who are you?" the creature asked.

"What are you?" Eli responded.

The creature sighed, annoyed.

"I am a night elf, you doltish human," he growled. "And you will die here tonight if you don't answer my questions."

"Right," Eli said. "I am E-"

Eli stopped. He thought this couldn't be real. He must be dreaming.

Night elves were something of video games and role-playing games, not real life.

But if this *was* real...

Eli racked his brain.

Never give a fae your real name.

"My name is Aeris Jagger," Eli gave the name of one of his video game characters. "I am the leader of the elf rangers of the forest."

The night elf tilted his head to one side and checked Eli's ears.

"You are not an elf, human," the night elf said. "You're lying, I can smell it."

"I didn't say I was an elf," Eli stammered slightly. "I said I was their leader."

The night elf narrowed his eyes at Eli.

"You are a leader of elves," the night elf scoffed.

Eli nodded.

"Then prove it," the night elf said.

"Prove it?" Eli asked. "How?"

"Summon your elves," the night elf said, brandishing his sword in the moonlight. "*Leader*."

"They're out on a mission," Eli said.

"Liar," the night elf scoffed.

"I'm not lying," Eli insisted.

"If you are a leader of elves," the night elf said. "Then you must be a master of weapons. You must join me on the Wild Hunt."

"What's the Wild Hunt?" Eli asked.

The night elf lowered his sword and stepped towards Eli. He pivoted slightly and gestured to the sky, "You saw the hunting party, running across the sky?"

Eli nodded, "Yes."

"That is the Wild Hunt," he said.

"Who were they?" Eli asked.

The night elf looked at him, amused, "They are the fae, the undead, and any creature that wants to join in on the hunt."

"What are they hunting?" Eli asked.

The night elf grinned, "You must come and find out for yourself."

Eli shook his head, "I don't think so."

"You, Aeris Jagger, have no choice but to join," the night elf said. "For anyone who has witnessed the Wild Hunt must join or die."

"Technically, that is a choice," Eli said.

The night elf turned faster than Eli could react and Eli felt the cold edge of the sword resting under his chin again.

"What is your choice, Aeris Jagger, leader of the elf rangers?" the night elf stared at Eli across the blade shimmering in the moonlight with his cold yellow eyes. They looked like a cat's eyes, with the black pupil wide in the darkness.

Eli felt a surge of bravery and he reached up and pushed the sword blade away from his chin with one carefully placed finger.

"I'll join," Eli said. "But I am not dressed for a hunt."

The night elf looked him up and down and turned towards the forest where he had been hiding, "Follow me."

*

Eli followed the night elf through the dark woods.

He had to almost jog because the night elf had much longer legs than he did, and his pace was quick. Eli didn't have time to listen to and enjoy the crunch of his boots in the snow, but he did notice that he was suddenly no longer in familiar territory.

He was in the woods, but they weren't his woods. It wasn't the woods near his home, where he knew the area well.

The trees were taller, denser. The woods were darker. Even with the full moon flickering in and out of the sky through the treetops that towered above them.

Eli felt like he was being watched. From everywhere. He couldn't shake the feeling that there were eyes on his constantly. And he could hear faint whispers among the trees as he passed.

As they made their way through the forest, Eli could feel his gait change. He looked down to see that he was wearing his green leather armor.

Not the pieced together armor that hung in his closet, waiting to be finished. It was the armor he dreamed of, that imaginary outcome that he wished he could create.

It had everything that he had imagined, down to the last detail.

The fur-lined cowl, the dark wool cape with highly detailed Celtic knots forged into the plate shoulder guards. The cape was heavy, but glided across the top of the snow with ease, keeping him surprisingly warm.

He had Celtic knotted metal wrist guards, fitted perfectly over heavy leather gloves. His hands felt warmer than they had in the gloves his mother had given him.

The lightweight green body armor that he had always imagined fit so well that it looked like clothing rather than armor. He almost tripped when he was trying to admire the quality and the fit while still trying to keep up with the night elf.

"Where are we going?" Eli asked, trying not to sound as winded as he felt.

His heavy leather boots with buckles and shin guards looked cool, but were getting heavier with every step.

"You'll see when we get there," the night elf said.

Strapped to his back, Eli could feel a longbow and a quiver of arrows. A sword dangled in a sheath on each side of his belt, and knives were hidden in all of the places he had imagined being able to hide a knife.

"Can you at least tell me your name?" Eli asked.

He could move surprisingly easily. Only occasionally getting poked or smacked by something hidden in his belt or boot or folds of his cape. He was just not used to the weight of the clothing. Leather and wool were heavy, not to mention the metal guards.

"You can call me Sagewalker," the night elf said.

"Sagewalker?" Eli repeated, trying to hide a laugh.

The night elf stopped and turned to face Eli, "Do you have a problem with my name?"

Eli stopped, and looked up at the night elf and into his creepy yellow eyes.

"No, none at all," Eli said. "I just repeat names so I don't forget them."

Sagewalker grunted and turned back to his path.

Eli continued to follow him.

"How much farther is it?" Eli asked.

Sagewalker turned and glared at him, "Do you talk this much with the day elves?"

"They tend to be," Eli paused slightly. "Friendlier."

"Not the ones I've met," Sagewalker growled.

Eli stood and stared at the night elf. He still couldn't believe this was real. He was waiting to wake up. To realize that all this had only been a dream.

But his face was too cold and his nose was running from the frigid night air. His nose was never runny and his face never hurt in his dreams.

He continued to follow the night elf for what seemed like it should be a long way. But they never seemed to get anywhere. Eli felt like they were passing the same landmarks over and over again.

"Are we going in circles?" Eli asked.

The night elf grinned back at him.

"You've passed the first test," Sagewalker said.

Eli stopped walking. "This was a test?"

"Yes," Sagewalker said. "It took you long enough, but you passed."

"I can't believe it," Eli stammered. "If I knew this was going to be a test."

"What?" Sagewalker mocked. "You would've studied?"

"I would've paid attention more," Eli said. "I thought you were just leading me somewhere."

"Always assume everything is a test," Sagewalker said. "Or at least don't blindly trust a stranger who is leading you somewhere unknown."

Eli just glared at him.

"Silly human," Sagewalker turned back to the path and started walking again.

"So, are we in phase two now?" Eli asked as he started following the night elf. "Are we starting the second test? Because this time, I'm ready."

Sagewalker laughed and kept walking.

Eli followed in silence. He was getting tired and this wasn't feeling like an adventure anymore. It felt like a hike. In weather that was too cold with a leader he didn't want to follow anymore.

The night was getting darker and colder and later, although the moon was still lighting the way as it moved across the sky.

When Eli finally felt like he just wanted to turn back, he heard something off in the distance.

"What is that?" Eli asked.

"Shhh," Sagewalker waved him to silence.

The two quietly ran over and hid behind some bushes and Sagewalker pointed to a clearing ahead of them.

"Watch," he whispered.

Eli focused his eyes on the clearing. His eyelids were feeling heavy and he was growing more and more tired. But he watched the clearing and waited.

The sounds were getting closer. It sounded like hundreds of voices and hooves beating on the ground. A crowd stampeding closer and closer. The ground started to feel like it was shaking beneath him.

As he watched the clearing, creatures of all sorts ran into sight. Hellhounds led the charge, barking and howling as they led the pack into the clearing. There were centaurs with their bows drawn and more night elves than he could count. There were all manner of creatures that Eli couldn't even identify. All were armed and all looked like they were chasing something. Hunting something. Ready to kill something.

The hellhounds screeched to a halt. Their jagged toothed mouths dripping slobber and blood. They had very little hair, but their bodies were tightly wound muscles, ready to pounce as soon as they caught wind of their prey.

Eli tried to remain quiet. He didn't even want to breathe for fear of the hellhounds catching his scent.

"Are you ready?" Sagewalker whispered.

"Ready for what?" Eli whispered back.

"To join the hunt," Sagewalker said.

"No," Eli changed his mind. "I'm good."

"It is join or die," Sagewalker said. "I will kill you right here in hiding, like the coward you are."

Eli sighed. "Whatever."

Sagewalker grinned at him, his yellow cat-like eyes gleaming in the moonlight. Eli suddenly felt like he should have never trusted the night elf.

Sagewalker grabbed Eli before he could react and twisted his arm behind his back. Sagewalker dragged Eli to his feet and pushed him out in front of him like a shield as he walked towards the armed and battle-ready crowd.

Eli watched in horror as the hellhounds locked their eyes on him and growled menacingly.

"My fellow huntsmen," Sagewalker yelled. "I have found my surety."

The entire hunting party was now staring at them. Sagewalker continued to hold Eli tightly in front of him. His grip was like iron and no matter what Eli did, he couldn't shake the night elf's grasp.

"What?" Eli said. "What's a surety?"

The hunting party made room for a man - a creature - that looked like something undead. He was extremely tall, dwarfing the centaurs as he passed them. His wrinkled and rotting skin was tinted a light blue in the moonlight and he was wearing animal furs over his leather and iron clad armor. He had an ax with a long handle and carried it like he was ready to swing it at any time. And he wore a crown on his head that looked like it was made of bones and ice.

His cold eyes felt like they were boring a hole through Eli.

Eli found it difficult to meet the creature's gaze.

"What is your name?" the creature said.

Eli tried to speak, but no words came.

"He said his name is Aeris Jagger," Sagewalker said.

The creature looked at Eli as if he were analyzing him. "He lies."

"He said he was the leader of elven rangers," Sagewalker said.

Eli felt himself grow colder with each step the creature took towards him. A cold that felt like it would never leave him. His bones felt like they were being covered with frost and he started to shiver uncontrollably in the creature's presence.

It only took the creature a few of his long-legged steps and he was in front of Eli, staring down at him.

Sagewalker loosened his grip on Eli.

"No one lies to me," the creature said.

"I-I was afraid to give a fae my real name," Eli stammered.

The creature chuckled, "You're smarter than you look."

"I-I also didn't agree to be a surety," Eli said.

"No one agrees to be a surety," the creature laughed. "You just are one."

"What?" Eli gasped. "Why?"

"Sagewalker was banded as a traitor," the creature said. "Killed one of our own."

"Accidentally," Sagewalker chimed in.

"There are no accidents," the creature snapped at the night elf.

He looked back to Eli, "His punishment was death, or bringing in a new quarry."

"That would be you," Sagewalker whispered over Eli's shoulder.

"Quarry?" Eli looked over at the crowd of hunters, who were staring at him like he was lunch and they hadn't eaten in days.

"I'm not quarry," Eli said. "I'm no one's quarry."

Eli reached back into his belt with his free hand and pulled a knife out from behind him. He pivoted around before the night elf knew what was happening and stabbed Sagewalker in the neck.

More blood than Eli ever expected spattered out onto the white snow. He stepped away and watched as Sagewalker fell lifeless between him and the ice creature.

Eli looked up at the creature in front of him. When he met the creature's eyes, it started to laugh.

Eli drew his swords. He knew it was futile, but the adrenaline coursing through his veins decided he wasn't going down without a fight.

"Hold," the creature put up a hand to stop Eli.

Eli stood in the snow, with the night elf still bleeding into the snow at his feet. His shivering had become almost violent, but he did all he could to stand his ground.

The creature grinned at Eli, "You have earned your way into the hunt."

"I'm no one's quarry," Eli almost shouted.

"No, you're certainly not," the creature said. "You are one of us now."

"What?" Eli said.

"There is no escape but death," the creature said to Eli. "You join the hunt, forever more, or you will freeze to death where you stand."

Eli could feel himself starting to succumb to the cold. He looked over at the hunting party in desperation. They stood in silence, waiting for his decision.

"Okay," Eli relented. "I'll join."

The creature held out his ax and touched Eli on each shoulder, "You will forevermore be Aeris Jagger, leader of the elf rangers, and member of the Wild Hunt."

Eli suddenly felt the cold melting away from his bones. He felt warmer, stronger.

He reached up to feel his ears, which had grown larger and to a point. His hearing was much better than he ever thought it could be. His vision sharper. And his sense of smell had heightened, much to his dismay.

"You can never return to your world," the creature said to him. "You are one of us now."

Eli looked down at the night elf, who was fading away into the snow, as if he never had been.

"Come, Aeris," the creature led him to the cheering party. "Tonight, we hunt."

www.ingramcontent.com/pod-product-compliance
Lightning Source LLC
Chambersburg PA
CBHW072110150726
47999CB00005B/1980